A LIFT-THE-FLAP BOOK

CORDUROY'S Sleepover

BASED ON THE CHARACTER CREATED BY DON FREEMAN
STORY BY B. G. HENNESSY • PICTURES BY LISA McCUE

SCHOLASTIC INC.
New York Toronto London Auckland Sydney
Mexico City New Delhi Hong Kong Buenos Aires

Corduroy is excited. Scruffy Pup just called and invited him to a sleepover party! What should Corduroy bring? He packs fuzzy slippers, a toothbrush, his favorite toy, a flashlight, a book, and pajamas.

Corduroy walks over to Scruffy Pup's house. Along the way, he meets Checkerboard Bunny and Blue Mouse. Do you need any help carrying your sleeping bag, Corduroy?

Scruffy Pup has a lot of games. Corduroy wants to play Checkers. Blue Mouse wants to play Go Fish. Checkerboard Bunny wants to play Pick Up Sticks. "Don't worry," says Scruffy Pup. "We have enough time to play *all* of them!"

After the games, Corduroy has an idea. "Let's build a fort!" Before long, the room is full of pillows and blankets. Corduroy gets his flashlight, and they make shadow puppets on the wall. "Look, it's a butterfly!" says Corduroy.

Now it's movie time. Scruffy Pup puts some popcorn in a big bowl.
This is Corduroy's favorite movie! When it's over, everyone is sleepy.

Corduroy and his friends put on their pajamas and brush their teeth. Then everyone snuggles into their sleeping bags.

Blue Mouse is wide awake. "It's so dark in here!" he says. Scruffy Pup turns on a nightlight. "I like a story and a song before bed," Blue Mouse says. Corduroy reads him a story, and Checkerboard Bunny sings a nighttime song. Blue Mouse cuddles up with his toy mouse, and soon the four friends are fast asleep. *Shhhhh!*

Don Freeman was born in San Diego, California, and moved to New York City to study art, making his living as a jazz trumpeter. Following the loss of his trumpet on a subway train, Mr. Freeman turned his talents to art full-time. In the 1940s, he began writing and illustrating children's books. His many popular titles include *Corduroy*, *A Pocket for Corduroy*, *Gregory's Shadow*, *Earl the Squirrel*, and *Fly High, Fly Low*.

B. G. Hennessy spent many years working in New York City as the art director for Viking Children's Books. One of the first books she worked on was Don Freeman's *A Pocket for Corduroy*. B. G. Hennessy is the author of over thirty children's books, including all of the Corduroy lift-the-flaps. You can learn more about her work at www.bghennessy.com. She now lives with her family in Paradise Valley, Arizona.

Lisa McCue has illustrated more than eighty books, including *Corduroy Goes to the Beach*, *Corduroy Goes to the Library*, *Corduroy's Thanksgiving*, and *Corduroy's Snow Day*. She lives in Annapolis, Maryland, with her husband and their two sons.

ISBN-13: 978-0-545-03944-4
ISBN-10: 0-545-03944-4

Text copyright © 2007 by Penguin Group (USA) Inc. Illustrations copyright © 2007 by Lisa McCue. All rights reserved. Published by Scholastic Inc., 557 Broadway, New York, NY 10012, by arrangement with Viking, a division of Penguin Young Readers Group, a member of Penguin Group (USA) Inc. SCHOLASTIC and associated logos are trademarks and/or registered trademarks of Scholastic Inc.

12 11 10 9 8 7 6 5 4 3 2 1   7 8 9 10 11 12/0
Printed in Malaysia   46
First Scholastic printing, October 2007
Set in Stempel Garamond